Pinny
in
Summer

~

JOANNE SCHWARTZ
ISABELLE MALENFANT

GROUNDWOOD BOOKS
HOUSE OF ANANSI PRESS
TORONTO   BERKELEY

Groundwood Books / House of Anansi Press
groundwoodbooks.com

We acknowledge for their financial support of our publishing
program the Canada Council for the Arts, the Ontario Arts
Council and the Government of Canada.

Canada Council   Conseil des Arts
for the Arts   du Canada

ONTARIO ARTS COUNCIL
CONSEIL DES ARTS DE L'ONTARIO
an Ontario government agency
un organisme du gouvernement de l'Ontario

With the participation of the Government of Canada
Avec la participation du gouvernement du Canada   Canadä

Library and Archives Canada Cataloguing in Publication
Schwartz, Joanne (Joanne F.), author
Pinny in summer / written by Joanne Schwartz ; illustrated
by Isabelle Malenfant.
Issued in print and electronic formats.
ISBN 978-1-55498-782-5 (bound).
— ISBN 978-1-55498-783-2 (pdf)
I. Malenfant, Isabelle, illustrator II. Title.
PS8637.C592 P56 2016   jC813'.6   C2015-903584-8
C2015-903585-6

The illustrations were done with soft pastel, graphite pencil,
Q-tips and an electric eraser.
Design by Michael Solomon
Printed and bound in Malaysia

to my mother, Diana,
with oceans of love
— JS

To my dear friend Billy
— IM

Pinny

Pinny stepped outside. Summer was almost over. Days and weeks of sunshine had passed slowly by. This morning the sun was shining again, making everything as warm as toast. Pinny was happy.

Pinny wandered down the path. She was looking for a special kind of rock. It had to have a stripe running all the way around it, for that would be a wishing rock. Pinny knew wishing rocks were very hard to find, but if she looked and looked, maybe she would find one. Then she could make a wish.

Pinny picked up lots of rocks. She found one with sparkly bits in it and another smooth, flat rock that fit perfectly in her hand. She found a rock with a whirly pattern on it and one that looked like the head of an arrow, but she didn't find a wishing rock.

On the way home, Pinny bumped into her friends Annie and Lou. They were carrying pails for blueberry picking.

"Perfect," said Pinny. "I'll come, too. If we pick enough blueberries, I'll make my wild blueberry cake and we can have a party to celebrate summer."

Big puffy clouds sailed across the sky. Seagulls swooped overhead, gliding up and down on the wind.

"Look at those clouds," said Pinny.

She lay down in the grass, and Annie and Lou did, too. The sky was enormous, and they all watched the clouds floating high above them. They saw clouds that looked like feathers and fish and dragons.

One cloud looked like a cake. It reminded them of the cake Pinny was going to bake. The three friends jumped up and headed off to Blueberry Hill.

Blueberry Hill was bursting with berries, and they had no trouble filling their pails. Pinny, Annie and Lou were so busy they didn't notice the breeze getting breezier and the clouds growing grayer. A sudden gust blew, and a dark cloud cast a shadow over the blueberry patch. Pinny looked up and a fat raindrop hit her on the nose.

"Oh no," said Pinny. "Let's run!"

The rain came down faster and faster. The friends raced down the path, berries spilling here and there. When they were almost home, Annie and Lou gave their pails to Pinny.

"We'll be over later for the party."

Pinny's shoes were so wet that she took them off and ran the rest of the way home, with her bare feet squelching in the soft, wet grass.

Pinny was tired from running all the way home. She curled up in a chair to read a book and dry off. She was enjoying her book so much she didn't hear the tapping at the window. When the tapping came again, Pinny thought it was someone at the door.

She hopped out of her chair and peered outside. No one was there. Pinny curled up in her chair and started to read again.

Tap, tap, tap.

This time Pinny knew the tapping was at her window. The largest seagull she had ever seen was standing there. The seagull tapped again and cocked his head to one side, as if to say, "Won't you say hello?"

Pinny slowly opened the window.

"Hello to you, too," she said.

The seagull opened and closed his beak.

Oh, thought Pinny. *Maybe he wants some food.* She got some bread, tore it into small pieces and put it on the window sill.

The seagull pecked away happily. When he was finished, he cocked his head to one side, as if to say, "Thank you." And then he flew away.

Pinny carried the cake out to the picnic table and went back inside to make a big pot of tea. Her friends would arrive soon, and she wanted to be all ready. The kettle came to a whistling boil, and she filled the teapot to the brim.

Just then, Pinny heard a big commotion. She went outside to find Annie and Lou jumping up and down and yelling, "Shoo, shoo!" to a very large seagull who was helping himself to the cake.

When the seagull saw Pinny, he cocked his head to one side, as if to say, "What a nice treat."

Pinny laughed. "I guess seagulls like wild blueberry cake, too!"

Pinny Has a Party

Clink, clink, clink went the dishes as Pinny prepared for her party. To make her wild blueberry cake, Pinny beat and mixed all the ingredients together and then she folded in the fresh blueberries. She poured the batter into the pan and put it in the oven.

When the cake had baked and cooled, Pinny piled whipped cream on top. She was so pleased with her cake that she did a little dance around the kitchen.

The seagull had eaten a big chunk of the cake, and now he hopped about the table, squawked loudly and flew off.

It was then that Pinny noticed a wishing rock on the table. She stuck her hand in her pocket and found it empty.

"Wow!" Pinny said for the second time that day. "I must have lost my wishing rock and the seagull has brought it back to me!"

"But what about your cake?" asked Annie.

"We have nothing for our party," said Lou.

"Sure we do," said Pinny. "I have lots of extra blueberries and whipped cream. We can feast on that and tomorrow I'll make my wild blueberry cake again."

The three friends enjoyed their feast as the evening rolled in. When it was time to go home, Annie and Lou and Pinny made plans to meet the next day to pick more blueberries.

The sky changed from blue, to a deeper blue, then to dark blue. Pinny held the wishing rock in her hand as she climbed into bed. She traced the white ring on the rock all the way around and closed her eyes.

"I wish for another perfect day tomorrow."

Pinny yawned and fell asleep.